Fishing

Tatiana Tomljanovic

Weigl

CALGARY
www.weigl.com

Published by Weigl Educational Publishers Limited
6325 10 Street SE
Calgary, Alberta T2H 2Z9

Library of Congress Cataloging-in-Publication Data

Tomljanovic, Tatiana
    Fishing / Tatiana Tomljanovic.

(Linking Canadian communities)
Includes index.
ISBN 978-1-55388-379-1 (bound)
ISBN 978-1-55388-380-7 (pbk.)

    1. Fisheries--Canada--Juvenile literature. 2. Fisheries--Economic
aspects--Canada--Juvenile literature. 3. Fisheries--Canada-- History--
Juvenile literature. I. Title. II. Series.
SH223.T65 2007   j338.3'7270971   C2007-902264-2

Printed in the United States of America
1 2 3 4 5 6 7 8 9 11 10 09 08 07

Editor
Heather C. Hudak
Design
Warren Clark

We acknowledge the financial support of the Government of Canada through the Book Publishing
Industry Development Program (BPIDP) for our publishing activities.

Contents

What is a Community?

A community is a place where people live, work, and play together. There are large and small communities.

Small communities are also called rural communities. These communities have fewer people and less traffic than large communities. There is plenty of open space.

Large communities are called towns or cities. These are urban communities. They have taller buildings and more cars, stores, and people than rural communities.

Canada has many types of communities. Some have forests for logging. Others have farms. There are also fishing, energy, **manufacturing**, and mining communities.

Types of Canadian Communities

FARMING COMMUNITIES
- use the land to grow crops, such as wheat, barley, canola, fruits, and vegetables
- some raise livestock, such as cattle, sheep, and pigs

ENERGY COMMUNITIES
- found near energy sources, such as water, natural gas, oil, coal, and uranium
- have **natural resources**
- provide power for homes and businesses

FISHING COMMUNITIES
- found along Canada's 202,080 kilometres of coastline
- fishers catch fish, lobster, shrimp, and other underwater life

Real Canadian Communities

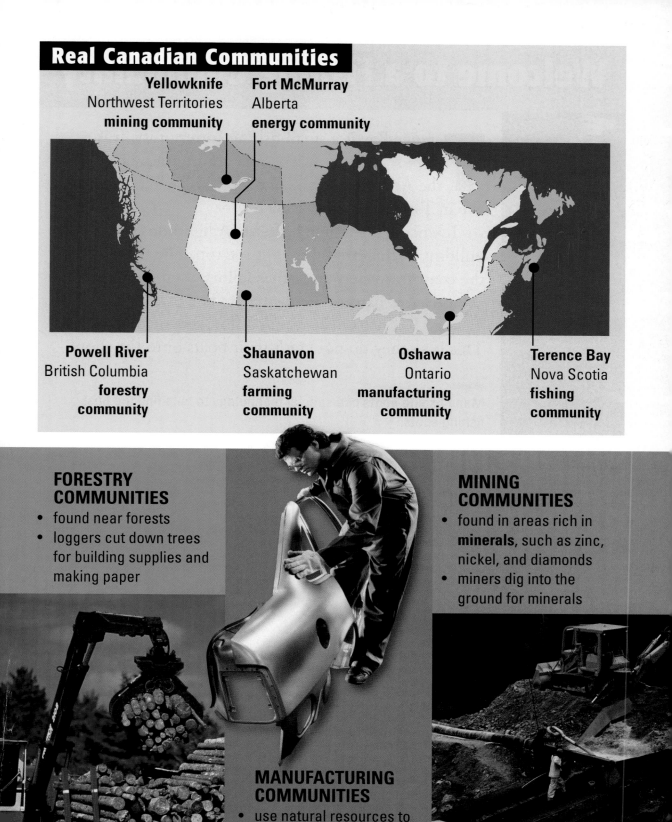

Yellowknife
Northwest Territories
mining community

Fort McMurray
Alberta
energy community

Powell River
British Columbia
**forestry
community**

Shaunavon
Saskatchewan
**farming
community**

Oshawa
Ontario
**manufacturing
community**

Terence Bay
Nova Scotia
**fishing
community**

FORESTRY COMMUNITIES
- found near forests
- loggers cut down trees for building supplies and making paper

MANUFACTURING COMMUNITIES
- use natural resources to make a finished product
- finished products include cars and computers

MINING COMMUNITIES
- found in areas rich in **minerals**, such as zinc, nickel, and diamonds
- miners dig into the ground for minerals

Welcome to a Fishing Community

Terence Bay is a small fishing community. It is in Nova Scotia. It is a rural community near the Atlantic Ocean. Many of the people who live in Terence Bay are fishers.

Terence Bay has a lighthouse. A lighthouse is a tall building with a bright light at the top. The light marks the coast for fishers and other sailors. At night or during a storm, it is hard to see the coast. The lighthouse in Terence Bay helps fishers and sailors see the rocky coast. This is so they do not crash their boats onto the shore.

Many fishing boats use special technology to help find the best fishing spots.

First-hand Account

My name is Matthew. I live in Terence Bay. My house is high on a hill near the ocean. From my bedroom window, I can watch the fishing boats. I see people from the village going to and from their boats. There are old log sheds around the docks. These are used for storing fish and repairing nets.

My dad is a fisher. He says that the ocean seems to be running out of fish. I wish my dad would let me go out on his boat with him. I would love to help him catch fish. Sometimes, my friends and I climb onto a huge rock by the ocean. We pretend to be fishers. We hold onto cords attached to toy boats. We let them float on the water.

There are small bays close to my home. There are other fishing villages like Terence Bay along the eastern coast of Canada. Many of the people who live there are fishers. In winter, the boats are pulled up on shore. Fishers find other jobs to do until spring.

Nova Scotia

Terence Bay

Atlantic Ocean

N   0   200   400 kilometres
     0   200   400 miles

Think About It

Compare Terence Bay to your community. Is the environment the same or different?
- **How is it the same?**
- **How is it different?**

The Fishing Industry

Fishers that catch fish and **shellfish** are part of the fishing industry. The fishing industry includes factories and other businesses. It **processes** fish and sells it to grocery stores and restaurants. About 130,000 Canadians work in the industry. People who live in communities on the coast fill many of these jobs.

The fishing industry is important to the Atlantic Provinces. Nova Scotia, New Brunswick, Newfoundland and Labrador, and Prince Edward Island are the Atlantic Provinces. These provinces depend on the fishing industry.

The fishing industry sells more than $1 billion of lobster each year.

Timeline

1534

Jacques Cartier discovers the Gulf of the St. Lawrence River. This begins Canada's fishing industry.

1734

Canada's first lighthouse is built.

1889

Fishing seasons are established to protect lobsters laying eggs.

Fishers work on boats. They lay traps and nets into the ocean to catch fish. There are many kinds of fishing. Trawling is one type of fishing. A net is dragged through the water behind a boat. Fish get caught in the nets.

Clam diggers look for clams under mud flats. They use a clam hack and a spading fork. Clam diggers push the mud down with the hack. They use the fork to pull up the clams. Some boats have a clam rake. At the end of the rake is a basket. The clams are collected in the basket. Some people have fish farms. This is called aquaculture. Fish are raised in tanks or enclosed areas.

Fishers use weirs, or large nets on stakes, to trap fish.

1924
The first fishers' **union** is created in Canada.

1973
Global Positioning System (GPS) is used for **navigation**.

1993
All Canadian cod fishing is banned to allow cod numbers to increase.

Lobster Processing

Most lobsters are caught within 15 kilometres of Canada's east coast. Fishers catch lobsters today the same way they did hundreds of years ago. They use lobster traps or pots to catch lobsters.

Lobster pots are made of wood or plastic-coated metal surrounded by rope mesh. The traps are placed on the bottom of the ocean floor. A piece of bait is put inside the trap. When a lobster enters the trap, it cannot leave. Fishers check the pots for lobsters every few days.

Fishers attach **buoys** to the pots. The buoys float above water. They mark where the lobster pots are in the ocean. This helps fishers find the pots later to check them for lobsters.

The lobsters are grouped by weight and size. Large lobsters are sold live in fresh markets. Small lobsters are processed in a factory. They are cleaned and cooked. Some lobsters are sold whole to people and businesses. Canada provides more than half the world's supply of lobster. Atlantic lobster is Canada's top seafood **export**.

Lobster pots do not catch as many lobsters as other fishing methods. However, they do not damage the ocean floor.

Lobster Processing

Fishers lay baited traps for lobsters.

Fishers check traps for lobsters.

Lobsters are weighed, measured, and marked.

Large lobsters are sold in fresh markets.

Small lobsters are processed or frozen.

Processed lobsters are cleaned and cooked. They may be left whole, cut into parts, or have the meat removed.

Processed, frozen, and live lobsters are shipped across Canada and the world.

Canada's Fishing Map

Canadian fishers catch salmon, cod, lobster, flounder, sole, halibut, and shellfish off Canada's Pacific and Atlantic coasts. A shellfish is an animal with a shell that lives in the water. There are many types of shellfish, such as lobster, shrimp, and crab. This map shows where different types of fish are caught off Canada's coasts.

Legend

- Pacific salmon
- Atlantic cod
- Lobster
- Flounder and sole
- Pacific halibut

U.S.A.

Yukon Territory

● Whitehorse

Northwest Territories

Nunavut

Yellowknife ●

C A N A D A

Alberta

Edmonton ●

Saskatchewan

British Columbia

Regina ●

Pacific Ocean

● Victoria

U N I T E D   S T A T E S
O F   A M E R I C A

N

0   500 kilometres
0   500 miles

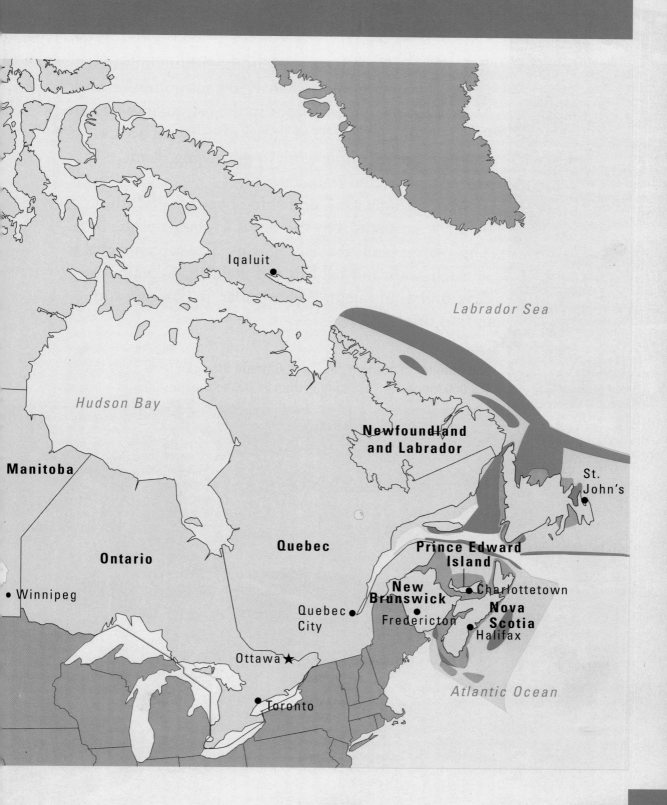

Iqaluit

Labrador Sea

Hudson Bay

**Newfoundland
and Labrador**

Manitoba

St.
John's

Ontario

Quebec

**Prince Edward
Island**

• Winnipeg

**New
Brunswick**

• Charlottetown

Quebec
City •

Fredericton •

**Nova
Scotia**

Halifax •

Ottawa ★

Atlantic Ocean

• Toronto

Careers

Many Canadians work in the fishing industry. People in more than 1,500 communities work in the industry. Jobs in the fishing industry are fishing boat captain, coast guard officer, and ocean scientist. Some people work in processing plants, grocery stores, and restaurants.

Many people work on fishing boats. Every fishing boat has a captain. The captain is in charge of the boat. This person plans the fishing trips. The captain's goal is to catch, trap, and sell fish and shellfish. Captains use electronic equipment, such as radar, to navigate and to find fish.

___

The amount of codfish caught in Canada dropped from more than 480,000 tonnes in 1988 to less than 24,000 tonnes in 2003.

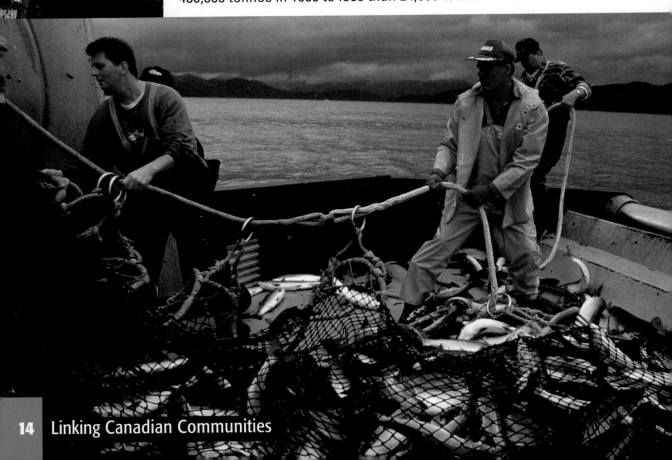

The Canadian Coast Guard is the police force of the ocean. The coast guard helps people who are in trouble. It protects the ocean from pollution and helps stop illegal overfishing. Overfishing happens when too many fish are caught each year and very few of a certain type of fish remain.

Ocean scientists study the ocean. Some ocean scientists work for the Department of Fisheries and Oceans Canada. They study the ocean's **climate** and record their findings. This research helps people better understand the ocean environment and the fish that live there.

Aquaculture is a new industry that breeds and raises fish in an artificial, or human-made, environment.

The Canadian Coast Guard helps ships find their way through fields of ice.

Think About It
What other jobs might there be in the fishing industry?

Links Between Communities

Everyone is part of a community. It may be a village, a town, or a city. Communities are linked to one another. Each Canadian community uses goods that link it to other communities. Goods are things people grow, make, or gather to use or sell.

A forestry community makes lumber for construction. The wood may be shipped to another community to build houses or furniture.

Energy communities produce natural gas, oil, and other types of energy, such as wind, solar, and hydro. Other communities use this energy to power their homes and vehicles.

Dairy products and meats come from farming communities that raise cattle and other animals. People in all communities drink milk products and eat meat from these communities. Many farming communities grow crops such as wheat. Wheat is used to make bread and pastries.

These goods may be fish, grains, cars, and paper products. Communities depend on one another for goods and services. A service is useful work that is done to meet the needs of others. People are linked when they use the goods and services provided by others.

Manufacturing communities make products such as cars and trucks. They also make airplanes, ships, and trains that are used to transport, or move, people and goods from one place to another. Transportation services help communities build links.

Fishing communities send fish to stores to be bought by people in other places. In Canada, most fish is caught off the Pacific or Atlantic coast. People living on farms or in cities across the country buy the fish at stores.

Diamonds, gold, and potash can be mined. These items are sent from mining communities to other parts of the country. A diamond might be set in a ring for a person in another community.

Think About It

In your community, what goods and services help meet your family's needs and wants?

The Environment and the Community

The fishing industry is important to Canada, especially to the Atlantic Provinces. The industry has become smaller due to overfishing. In 1992, the **stocks** of Canadian cod were very low. A year later, the government banned cod fishing. There has been no cod fishing for 15 years. Still, there are few cod. The Canadian government tries to stop overfishing. Canada was one of the first countries in the world to protect fish stocks and ocean environments.

More than 14,000 Canadians work in the aquaculture industry.

Think About It

Could farmed fish one day replace traditional fishing?

Aquaculture is growing. It is found in each province and territory in Canada. In 2001, it made more than 20 percent of the total value of Canadian fish and seafood. By 2030, aquaculture may supply half of the fish and seafood eaten around the world. Today, it raises salmon, trout, Arctic char, blue mussels, and oysters.

Eco-friendly Aquaculture

Aquaculture experts are working on raising halibut and cod. This cod could be used to help increase cod stocks in the Atlantic Ocean. Over time, aquaculture farms may replace all of the sea life that was overfished.

Brain Teasers

Test your knowledge by trying to answer these brain teasers.

Q *Why do fishers need lighthouses?*

A Fishers need lighthouses so they can locate the coast at nighttime or during a storm and not crash into it.

Q *Name three types of communities in Canada.*

A Canada has forestry communities, farming communities, fishing communities, energy communities, and mining communities, and manufacturing communities.

Q *What two things link communities?*

A Goods and services link different communities together.

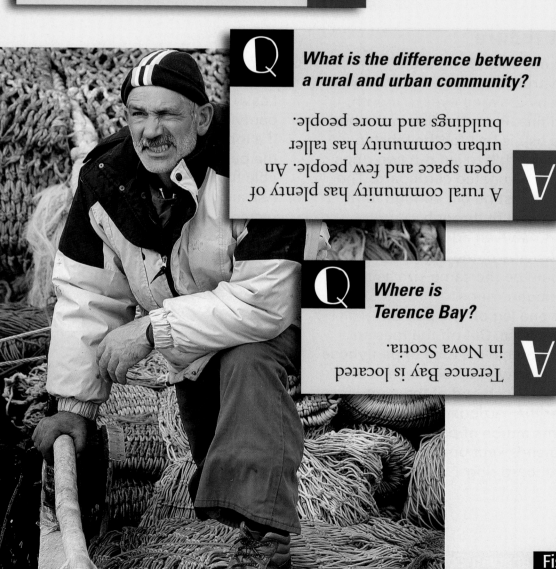

Q What are the main types of fish and shellfish that Canadian fishers catch?

A Canadian fishers catch salmon, cod, lobster, flounder, sole, and halibut.

Q What is the difference between a rural and urban community?

A A rural community has plenty of open space and few people. An urban community has taller buildings and more people.

Q Where is Terence Bay?

A Terence Bay is located in Nova Scotia.

Build a Lobster Pot

Fishers catch lobsters using wooden traps called lobster pots. Large lobsters can get into the trap, but they cannot get out. A small hole in the side of the trap allows small fish and baby lobsters to escape. Fishers put bait into the trap. You can build your own lobster pot at home.

Materials

- cardboard box with lid
- old pair of pantyhose
- scissors
- corrugated cardboard
- construction paper
- felt marker
- tape

Procedure

1. Cut out a fish from the construction paper. Decorate your fish by drawing eyes, a mouth, and fins. Place the fish in the box. The fish is bait for the lobster.
2. Ask an adult to cut out two rings from corrugated cardboard. The rings must be big enough for a lobster to fit through.
3. Next, have an adult cut a hole in the side of the box. The hole should be the same size as the cardboard rings.
4. Cut one leg off the pair of pantyhose. Cut off the toes so that you have a tube of pantyhose material with a hole in each end.
5. Stretch each end of the pantyhose over the cardboard rings. This forms a tube of pantyhose with two ends kept open by the cardboard rings.
6. Attach one cardboard ring to the hole in the box with tape.
7. Leave the other ring and pantyhose tube inside the box. If a lobster enters the box through the pantyhose tube, it will not be able to get out.
8. Ask an adult to cut out a small rectangle-shaped hole in your box. The hole is an escape vent for baby lobsters. Now you can show your friends, class, and parents how a lobster pot works!

Further Research

Many books and websites provide information on energy communities. To learn more about energy communities, borrow books from the library, or surf the Internet.

Books

Most libraries have computers that connect to a database for researching information. If you input a key word, you will be provided with a list of books in the library that contain information on that topic. Non-fiction books are arranged numerically, using their call number. Fiction books are organized alphabetically by the author's last name.

Websites

The World Wide Web is also a good source of information. Reliable websites usually include government sites, educational sites, and online encyclopedias.

To learn more about the Canadian fishing industry, visit Fisheries and Oceans Canada at **www.dfo-mpo.gc.ca**.

Find out more about Canada's lobster at **http://atn-riae.agr.ca/seafood/lobster-e.htm**.

Check out Nova Scotia by looking at photos and reading about the government, the people, and the province at **www.gov.ns.ca**.

Words to Know

buoys: floating markers anchored to the ocean floor

climate: average weather conditions of a place throughout the year

export: to send goods to another country to sell them

Global Positioning System: a system that uses signals from satellites in space to find objects on Earth

manufacturing: making a large amount of an item using machines

minerals: inorganic substances that are obtained through mining

natural resources: materials found in nature, such as water, soil, and forests, that can be used by people

navigation: the science of figuring out the position and course of ships

processes: the series of steps or actions taken to make a new product

shellfish: shelled water animals, such as mollusks and crustaceans, that can be eaten as food

stocks: supplies or the amount of something that is available to use in the future

union: an organization or group that helps protect the rights of workers

Index